SPACE RAP

Steve Barlow and Steve Skidmore

Illustrated by Santy Gutiérrez

LONDON·SYDNEY

Franklin Watts
First published in Great Britain in 2019 by The Watts Publishing Group

Credits
Series Editor: Adrian Cole
Project Editor: Katie Woolley
Consultant: Jackie Hamley
Designer: Cathryn Gilbert
Illustrations: Santy Gutiérrez

HB ISBN 978 1 4451 5973 7
PB ISBN 978 1 4451 5974 4
library ebook ISBN 978 1 4451 5975 1

Printed in China

Franklin Watts
An imprint of
Hachette Children's Group
Part of The Watts Publishing Group
Carmelite House
50 Victoria Embankment
London EC4Y 0DZ

An Hachette UK Company
www.hachette.co.uk

www.franklinwatts.co.uk

THE BADDIES

Lord and Lady Evil

Dr Y

They want to rule the galaxy.

THE GOODIES

Boo Hoo   Jet   Tip

They want to stop them.

"We are listening to Space Rap," said Tip.

"It is ace!" said Boo Hoo.

"It is way too loud!" said Jet. "Someone will hear us."

Tip smiled. "No way! In space, no one can hear you rap!"

BOOM!

BOOM!

11

Jet was very angry. "Turn the music off!"

"I already have," replied Tip.

"Then what is that noise?"

"The alarm!" said Boo Hoo. "We have been spotted."

"Oh great!" said Jet. "You said no one would hear us."

"I was wrong," said Tip.

"It's the baddies!" said Boo Hoo.

"We're doomed!" cried Jet.

BARP! BARP!

13

The baddies attack!

Shawn hid.

The baddies shot by.

"Now what do we do, Boo Hoo?"

asked Tip.

Seconds later, a voice replied, "What's wrong?"

Tip told him.

"Hold on! I'm on my way!" said the voice.

The ship docked.

"He will save us!" said Tip.

"Let him in," said Jet.

The door opened.

Tip held out his hand. "Hello, Master... Oh!"

"Who are you?" said Tip.

"I'm Grandmaster Boss. The best rap star in space!"

Jet shook her head. "You got the wrong Boss, Tip!"

"I love your music," said Boo Hoo.

"Then I'll play some," said Grandmaster Boss.

"No!" wailed Jet.

Got you!

"We're doomed!" said Jet.

Grandmaster Boss smiled. "Don't worry.
We can turn up the beat! Hit it!"

29

ALBANIAN MAFIA WARS

THE RISE OF EUROPE'S DEADLIEST NARCOS

JOHN LUCAS